DEC 0 2 2021

Look-Alike Animals

IS IT A HONEYBEE OR A WASP?

by Susan B. Katz

PEBBLE
a capstone imprint

Pebble Sprout is published by Pebble, an imprint of Capstone.
1710 Roe Crest Drive
North Mankato, Minnesota 56003
www.capstonepub.com

Library of Congress Cataloging-in-Publication Data
Names: Katz, Susan B., 1971- author.
Title: Is it a honeybee or a wasp? / by Susan B. Katz.
Description: North Mankato, Minnesota : Pebble, [2022] | Series: Look-alike animals | Audience: Ages 5-8 | Audience: Grades K-1 | Summary: "Buzz! Buzz! Was that a honeybee or wasp zipping past your ear? While both yellow-and-black striped insects can cause a painful sting, they have many differences. Explore the many similarities and differences in this picture book from the Look-Alike Animal series. Early learners will be captivated by the engaging text and vibrant photographs"-- Provided by publisher.
Identifiers: LCCN 2021002408 (print) | LCCN 2021002409 (ebook) | ISBN 9781663908636 (hardcover) | ISBN 9781663908605 (pdf) | ISBN 9781663908629 (kindle edition)
Subjects: LCSH: Honeybee—Juvenile literature. | Wasps—Juvenile literature. Classification: LCC QL568.A6 K374 2022 (print) | LCC QL568.A6 (ebook) | DDC 595.79/9—dc23
LC record available at https://lccn.loc.gov/2021002408
LC ebook record available at https://lccn.loc.gov/2021002409

Image Credits
Getty Images: proxyminder, 26; Science Source: Cheryl Power, 12 (bottom); Shutterstock: Andy.M, 3, Anna_Kova (design element), cover (middle) and throughout, Danny Radius, 31, Dev_Maryna, 30, Ed Phillips, 6, ETgohome, cover (top), HollyHarry, 23, IanRedding, 17, 29, Jennifer Bosvert, 16, Karen Faljyan, 18, kojihirano, 15, Kuttelvaserova Stuchelova, 11, Lehrer, 25, Luc Pouliot, 8, Macronatura.es, 5, McCarthy's PhotoWorks, 24, Mirko Graul, 12 (top), Nadim Mahmud–Himu, 22, Natalia Bachkova, 10, 13, nonupperuct, 28, Pavel Krasensky, cover (bottom), PhoenixNeon, 7, Robert Keresztes, 19, rtbilder, 20, Ruksutakarn studio, 9, Scherbinator, 21, Sean McVey, 27, stopabox, 14, Teodor Costachioiu, 4

Editorial Credits
Editor: Christianne Jones; Designer: Elyse White; Media Researcher: Svetlana Zhurkin; Production Specialist: Laura Manthe

Printed and bound in the United States of America. PO4270

Honeybees and **wasps** are cousins. Both are **flying, stinging insects** that are part of the same family.

They might look alike, but they are different. Their **similarities** and **differences** are something to **buzz about!**

honeybee

Both
honeybees
and wasps

have **black** and yellow stripes

and wings. But honeybees might have

orange, golden, or amber stripes

mixed in with black ones.

Wasps aren't as colorful.

They only have bright

yellow and **black** stripes.

wasp

What's the buzz on the fuzz?

Honeybees are **fuzzy** or **hairy**.

But don't try to pet them!

honeybee

wasp

Wasps usually have **smooth** and **shiny** skin. You don't want to try and touch them either.

Wasps are **smaller** at the **waist.** This helps them fly **faster** than honeybees. Honeybees have **rounder bodies** and move **slower** from flower to flower.

wasp

Both insects have **four wings.** But wasp wings are **long** and **skinny.** Honeybee wings are **short** and **rounded.**

honeybee

wasp

Look at those legs!

You can tell the difference between wasps and honeybees by whether or not you see their legs while they fly. Do you see all of their **legs dangling** down?

Then it's a wasp!

honeybee

If the legs are mostly **hidden** when it's flying, **it's a honeybee!**

honeybee stinger

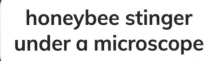

honeybee stinger
under a microscope

Female honeybees and wasps can sting. But honeybees have a **barbed stinger.**

When the honeybee tries to leave, her stinger gets **stuck.** Since it's attached to her body, she dies. That is why honeybees can sting only **one** time. Wasps can sting **multiple** times.

wasp stinger

Spread out your blanket but

watch out for wasps!

Wasps are drawn to **human food.** You might see them flying around your picnic.

wasp

honeybee

Honeybees

usually **float around flowers** and are a lot less likely to sting you.

honeybee

Honeybees **gather pollen** from flowers and make it into **honey** to **feed their young.** They don't kill or eat other insects.

Wasps like to eat **caterpillars, grasshoppers,** and **flies.** They do sip **nectar,** and fruit **juice,** from time to time. But wasps love to pick at **people food.**

wasp

With lots of honey, a hive is a big target for **bears, skunks,** and **hive beetles.**

Other honeybee predators include **crab spiders.** They hide out on flowers waiting for bees to land and then **gobble them up!**

a spider eating a honeybee

a praying mantis eating a wasp

Wasp predators include **dragonflies, centipedes, praying mantises,** and **moths.**

HONEY, I'M HOME!

honeybee hive

Honeybees live in a **hive** and **make honey.** The hives look like a honeycomb. Sometimes the hives hang from trees or are in tree trunks.

Wasps build **nests** and live in **colonies** underground, in hollow logs, or under the eaves of a roof.

wasp nest

honeybee colony

Sharing

a room with one person can be **tough.** Think about sharing your room with **thousands.**

Honeybee colonies can include more than **75,000** bees!

Wasp colonies

usually have less than

10,000

wasps in them.

wasp colony

Wasp and honeybee species with **queens** are called

social insects.

They live in **large groups** and **work together.**

a queen wasp

a queen honeybee

The queen is the only one that can **lay eggs** to make more bees or wasps. A queen honeybee can lay up to **1,500 eggs per day.**

a worker bee
feeding the queen

There are **different jobs** for honeybees within a **hive** and wasps within a **nest.**

The **queen** is the **top job.** Some workers **fan** the queen with their wings to keep her cool. Others **carry** in the queen's food.

Still more are **guards,** keeping away enemies like hornets and invading insects.

wasps guarding the nest

Brrr!

It's getting cold outside, but honeybees do not **hibernate** in winter. The worker bees form a **cluster** around the **queen bee.**

The cluster keeps them warm. Many worker honeybees die protecting the queen.

honeybee queen

wasp
queen

Most wasps die in winter.

But the **wasp queen**

hibernates

and comes out in **spring.**

honeybee

Honeybees **pollinate** plants and flowers, which helps much of our food grow. From strawberries to corn to watermelon, bees help **make our food.**

Wasps get a bad reputation because of their sharp sting, but they do **help the environment.**

Social wasps **eat pests** like flies and caterpillars. They also **pollinate** flowers.

wasp

IS IT A HONEYBEE OR A WASP?

1. An insect lands on your sandwich. Is it a honeybee or a wasp?

2. You see a fuzzy gold and black insect inside a flower. Is it a honeybee or a wasp?

3. It has a barbed stinger. Is it a honeybee or a wasp?

4. Its nest is hanging under your roof. Is it a honeybee or a wasp?

5. Its long legs are hanging down while it flies. Is it a honeybee or a wasp?

Answer Key:
1. wasp 2. honeybee 3. honeybee 4. wasp 5. wasp